Own Goal!

FOOTBALL MAD

Own Goal!

PAUL STEWART

Illustrated by
Michael Broad

Barrington Stoke

First published in 2020 in Great Britain by
Barrington Stoke Ltd
18 Walker Street, Edinburgh, EH3 7LP

www.barringtonstoke.co.uk

This story was first published in a different form
as *Football Mad* (Scholastic, 1997)

Text © 2020 Paul Stewart
Illustrations © 2020 Michael Broad

A CIP catalogue record for this book is available
from the British Library upon request

ISBN: 978-1-78112-930-2

Printed in China by Leo

To Reuben Raywood,
who loves football and reading

Chapter 1

"To me, to me, to me!" yelled Jack as Scott took control of the ball.

But, as always, Scott was trying to be too clever. With less than three minutes of the match left, there was just too much to lose. The score was 2–1 to Dale Juniors, but if they wanted to stay ahead – and win the cup – they needed to hold tight and play safe.

Jack watched the Weston players in their green and white shirts racing to the goal. His heart began to pound. They were closing in. It was already too late for Scott to pass.

"Back to Danny!" Jack shouted.

Danny stood in the goal watching Scott. He didn't like what he saw. One red shirt surrounded by stripes. Why didn't Scott just clear the ball?

"Get rid of it!" Danny screamed.

But Scott had got himself boxed in. He looked up at the two Weston players speeding towards him.

"Piece of cake," he muttered as he dribbled the ball slowly forwards.

He managed to wrong-foot their number 4, then slipped it past the number 2.

Magic! he thought.

But then, disaster! Before Scott could kick the ball away, Weston's number 7 came out of nowhere. He got his toe to the ball. Scott watched as it skidded out of his control.

Now things were really serious. Scott rushed forward. He back-heeled the ball and took back possession. But Weston's number 4 was behind him. Scott spun round and dribbled the ball past him. He still had control.

"Pass it!" Danny yelled.

Scott saw all three Weston forwards crowding in on him. There was no way there could be a throw-in now, and he didn't want to give away a corner.

"TO ME!" he heard Danny scream.

Scott had to admit that he had no other choice. Three against one was too much. He looked up, nodded at Danny and toe-punted the ball towards him.

At least, that's what he had wanted to do.

Perhaps it was the pressure that made things go wrong; perhaps the wind caught the ball. Whatever. As players and spectators looked on, the ball flew over Danny's arms, hit the nearside post and rebounded into the net.

Scott had scored an own goal.

The next moment the ref blew the final whistle. It was all over.

"You idiot," Jack groaned.

The final score was a sickening 2–2 draw. There would have to be a replay – the return match to be held away at Weston.

The boys of Dale Juniors made their way to the changing rooms with their heads down. So near yet so far. And all because of Scott! As Wes Hunter walked past, he paused and slapped Scott on the back.

"Nice one," he hissed.

"Yeah," Max Novak jeered. "Brilliant goal. *Captain.*"

"Perhaps it's time we had a new captain," Luke Edwards added, and the rest of the team muttered their agreement.

Scott had let everyone down. He felt sick.

Chapter 2

Jack Taggart. Danny Thompson. Scott Marley. The three of them were the best of mates. They wore the same brand of trainers, they rode the same make of bike, they listened to the same kind of music. They all liked computer games, cheeseburgers and ketchup; they all disliked books, girls and any green vegetables.

But they all *loved* football.

Every evening after school – winter and summer, rain and shine – they met up over the rec. At the far end, someone had painted goalposts on the wall. It was here that the three of them spent hours playing Corner.

They took it in turns. First Jack would float the ball over towards the goal, and Scott would try to head it or volley it past Danny. Then it was Scott's go to kick the ball to Jack. It was a pretty simple game, but they never got bored of it. In fact, if it hadn't been for school, they might have spent all their time at the rec.

Sadly for them there *was* school. Six hours a day, five days a week! Time when they couldn't play football. Time when they couldn't even talk tactics.

The only good thing about school was the football team. Scott was captain. Danny had proposed him and Jack had seconded. Scott had steered the team to the top of the local league and into the cup final. As the game had got nearer, everyone had been dreaming of winning the cup.

But for now, at least, that dream was over.

*

As the three boys lived on the same estate, they went to school and came home together. But that afternoon was different.

What Scott had done on the football pitch that afternoon had pushed the boys' friendship to the limit. Scoring an own goal was the ultimate no-no. After his shower, Scott Marley walked home alone.

Chapter 3

Scott felt truly awful – worse even than when his dog, Striker, had got run over. For the first time ever, Dale had been on the verge of winning the Langton Town Junior Cup, and *he* had messed it all up. Now he'd have to wait another two weeks for the replay to make good.

As he plodded slowly home, he kept going over the moment when the ball had crashed into the net. There was Danny, standing waiting for the ball. Just a little push, that was all it had needed. But Scott hadn't pushed it, had he? He'd kicked it.

Hard!

When he got home at last, Scott turned the key in the lock and opened the front door. The house was silent. His mum must have got held up at work again. That was good. Scott hadn't been looking forward to telling her what had happened.

He chucked his kit-bag down in the corner and went upstairs. He slammed his bedroom door shut, threw himself on to his bed and lay there staring up at the ceiling. He remembered the look on Danny's face as the ball came at him so fast. Scott shut his eyes. But the face wouldn't go away.

"I never even said sorry," he muttered to himself.

The downstairs clock chimed six. Scott sat up. On every other day, this was the signal for him to change into his football strip and head up to the rec.

They probably won't bother this evening, he thought.

All around him, the football heroes he had stuck to the wall stared back at him.

Scored an own goal, they seemed to be saying. *And he didn't even say sorry.*

Perhaps they will *be there*, Scott thought as he swung his feet down onto the carpet. *I'll go and see. Try to make it up to Danny somehow. I could lend him* Shoot Out. *He'd like that …*

Ten minutes later, Scott was standing at the gates of the rec. He looked around. Apart from a couple of younger kids playing on the swings, there was no one there.

Perhaps they're just late, he thought. *I'll give them a few minutes.*

He threw the ball down and began to dribble it across the grass. He ran fast, pretending to take the ball past this player, that player. It worked like a dream. It was as if the ball was glued to his feet. No one  could take it away from him. No one could stop him. And all around, the crowd roared him on.

"Scott! Scott! Scott!"

He dummied to the left and sprinted forwards. Scott closed in for the kill. He looked up quickly, tapped the ball with his left foot, lined himself up and ...

"*No!*" he screamed.

He'd miskicked the ball and missed by a mile. But Scott didn't notice. He stopped and stared at the wall, mouth open.

"How could he?" he muttered. He clenched his teeth and fought back the tears. "How *could* he?"

Above the bar of the painted goal was some new graffiti. The message was in bright red spray paint:

SCOTT MARLEY IS A MORONE!

Scott read it. He read it again. He felt more and more angry. It was in Danny's handwriting. But how could Danny do something like that? And he hadn't even spelled the word "moron" right.

"You couldn't say it to my face, could you?" Scott yelled. "You dirty, rotten ... *chicken*!"

Everyone in the park heard him. The kids on the swings looked up, and Scott saw they were laughing. Perhaps they'd already seen the graffiti. Pretty soon, everyone else would see it too.

He'd be nothing but a joke!

Chapter 4

When Jack and Danny walked into the changing room the following afternoon, the whole place went silent. Danny felt nine pairs of eyes staring at him.

"What is it?" he said. He felt his stomach churn. "Look, you can't blame me for what happened yesterday," he said. "I couldn't have saved that shot."

Still no one said a word. Wes Hunter sniggered.

"What is it?" Danny said again.

It was Jack who saw the blackboard first. Their coach – Mr Croft – planned match tactics on it. Jack tapped Danny on the arm and nodded towards the board. Laughter filled the room. Danny turned and stared.

There, in yellow chalk, was a message. Short, sweet and nasty:

DANNY THOMPSON IS A CHICKEN!

Danny felt sick. His scalp prickled. He looked at the grinning faces all around him.

"Who wrote that?" he asked.

Scott folded his arms and leaned back against the wall. "I did," he said. "What are you going to do about it?"

The room fell silent again.

"You?" said Danny, puzzled. "*You!* After what you did yesterday ... Why?"

"Don't come it, Danny. You know why," said Scott.

"I don't!"

"You're lying," Scott snapped.

"I am not lying," Danny shouted, and made a move towards Scott. Jack grabbed his arm.

"Just ignore it," he said softly.

Scott turned to the rest of the boys and smirked. "Of course Danny's going to deny it, isn't he?" he said. "Being a chicken!" he added, and he clucked like a hen.

This was too much for Danny. He pulled his arm free and threw himself across the room at Scott. He crashed into him and dragged him from the bench. The two of them fell to the floor, where they fought, each trying to pin the other down.

Everyone else in the changing room jumped up. They made a circle around Scott and Danny as the two of them rolled over and over across the floor.

"Come on, Scott!" someone shouted.

"Smack him, Danny!" yelled someone else.

Egged on by the sound of the cheering, jeering voices, Danny and Scott fought even harder. They sprawled around on the floor, arms and legs thrashing wildly. They pulled themselves up and threw wild punches. Then they fell back together and slammed hard into the central row of lockers.

For a second, the lockers hung at a crazy angle – the next second gravity took over and they fell to the floor with an almighty crash. Max Novak only just missed being crushed.

Suddenly the side-door burst open. It was Mr Croft, and he had a face like thunder.

"What do you two boys think you're doing?" he bellowed. He grabbed them both by their shirt collars and pulled them apart. Scott and Danny glared at one another.

"He started it," Danny mumbled.

"I'm not interested in who started it," said Mr Croft. "And after yesterday, don't you two think you've done enough already?"

Mr Croft waited. He looked at the two boys in turn. "If you're going to win that cup, you must play as a team," he said. "And a team," he added, fixing his gaze on Scott, "means eleven players. Not just one. A captain must understand that – if he's going to stay captain. Do you understand me?"

Scott looked down at the floor. "Yes, sir," he said.

Mr Croft nodded. "Now," he said, "I want these lockers stood up, then all of you outside. Three laps of the field." He turned back to Scott and Danny. "As for you two, you can both go and see Mr Lawson."

Mr Lawson! He was their headmaster. Scott and Danny couldn't believe it. Mr Lawson hated fighting. He handed out detentions and 200-word essays about "Why I must not fight in school". Worst of all, he sent letters home to parents.

Neither Scott nor Danny wanted any of that.

*

Ten minutes later, Danny and Scott stood on opposite sides of the corridor waiting for the headmaster to call them in. Scott was very nervous. It wasn't the first time he'd been sent to see Mr Lawson.

"This is all your fault," he hissed.

"Mine?" Danny whispered back. "You called me a chicken."

"You called me a moron," Scott replied hotly.

"I did not," said Danny.

"You did!"

"I didn't!"

"You *did*!"

Their voices were getting louder.

"When?" Danny asked.

"You know when," Scott snapped back.

"I do not!" Danny shouted.

Scott turned round. "Shut up," he hissed. "We're in enough trouble as it is."

Danny said nothing. He knew Scott was right. You had to stand outside the head's office in silence. That was the rule. But Danny couldn't stay silent.

"Just tell me what you think I've done," he whispered.

Scott didn't reply.

"Tell me!" Danny demanded.

And, at last, Scott explained about the message above the painted goalposts. Danny shook his head. He understood why Scott was angry. It was a mean thing to do. But *he* hadn't done it.

"I didn't even go up the rec yesterday," Danny said.

There was a moment of silence. Then Scott spoke. "I don't believe you," he said.

"Why not?" Danny shouted.

"Because it was in your writing!" Scott shouted back. "You were too chicken to say it to my face yesterday, and you're too chicken to admit it now. I hate you, Danny Thompson. You're pathetic!"

"And you're a stupid—"

At that moment, the door burst open.

"I believe you both know the rule concerning silence," Mr Lawson said in a soft voice.

Both boys looked at their feet. That was the worst thing about Mr Lawson – he never lost his cool. When he was angry, he spoke softly. The more angry he got, the softer he spoke, until he was almost whispering. And when Mr Lawson started whispering, you knew you were for it.

"Scott," he said, his voice like ice. "Follow me into my office. Daniel. Wait here. I'll deal with you later."

Chapter 5

It was four o'clock before Mr Lawson had finished with the two boys. Scott set off at once on his bike. Danny walked slowly out of the school gates. Jack was waiting for him.

"So, what happened?" he said at once.

"Well," said Danny. "For a start, we've both got to stay behind after school on Friday ..."

"And?"

Danny groaned. "He's writing to our parents."

"Oh, what?" said Jack. "Your dad's going to go crazy!"

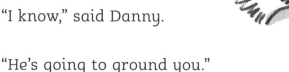

"I know," said Danny.

"He's going to ground you."

"I *know*!" Danny snapped. He turned away and stomped off along the pavement.

Jack ran to catch up. "Sorry," he said. "I didn't mean to rub it in."

Danny gave a shrug. He didn't slow down. And when he got to the T-junction, rather than turning right towards his house, he turned left.

"Where are you going?" asked Jack.

"Scott said there's some message been written up the rec," he shouted back. "He reckons I wrote it. I'm going to have a look."

"Up the rec?" Jack said as he trotted after Danny. "But I didn't think you went there yesterday."

"I didn't," said Danny. "That's what I kept telling him."

"And what did it say, this message?" asked Jack.

Danny sniggered. "Something about him being a moron."

"A moron!" Jack laughed. "Well, he is!"

"I know!" Danny said. "He's an idiot."

"A half-wit!"

"Brain like a stegosaurus," said Danny.

"Brain like a banana!" said Jack.

"Banana Brain!" they both growled together, and began laughing all over again.

Danny stopped laughing when they walked through the gates of the rec and he saw the red paint on the wall. He didn't say anything. They continued walking over the pitch. Halfway across, the words suddenly stood out. When Danny read the graffiti, he froze to the spot. His heart was racing.

"It does *look* like your writing," said Jack slowly.

"I can see that," said Danny. "I suppose you don't believe me now either."

"That's not what I said," said Jack. "But ..."

Danny turned on him. "Look, loads of people do their As like triangles," he said angrily.

He walked closer to the splash of graffiti. The thing was, everything about the writing made it look as if it was his. The triangular A, the loopy L, the backward Y. Danny began to think that maybe he *had* written it after

all! Was he losing his marbles? Had he done it without knowing? It was like some crazy dream.

"If *you* didn't write it ..." Jack began.

"I didn't!" Danny shouted. "Apart from anything else, I know how to spell 'moron'."

"OK, OK!" said Jack. "But whoever *did* write it wanted to make it look as if you'd done it."

Danny nodded.

"The question is," Jack went on, "why?"

"I've been thinking about that too," said Danny. "You remember when we voted for who should be captain?"

Jack nodded. "You proposed Scott. I seconded him," he said. "And he won easily."

"Yeah," said Danny. "But not everyone voted for him. There were three votes against. What if one of those three wants to get rid of Scott as captain—"

"And become captain himself!" Jack exclaimed.

"Exactly," said Danny. "So, who voted against?"

"There was Max," said Jack slowly.

"And Wes," said Danny.

"And Luke Edwards," they both said together.

"But which one do you think it is?" said Jack.

"That," said Danny grimly, "is what I intend to find out."

Chapter 6

"Come on," said Jack, and he turned to go. "There's nothing more we can do here."

At that moment, someone shouted over from the far end of the rec. Danny looked round. It was Scott. He was on his bike and pedalling towards them fast. Hanging from the handlebars was a small tin of paint; in his hand was a brush.

"Back at the scene of the crime, eh?" he said as he skidded to a stop next to them. He glared at Danny. "You've got a nerve, coming here," he said.

"It's a free country," said Jack.

"Who asked you?" said Scott angrily. He turned back to Danny. "You still reckon you didn't write it?"

"I didn't!" said Danny.

Scott turned away in disgust. "You make me sick," he said. He grabbed the paint pot, let his bike clatter to the grass and marched over to the wall. "Chicken!"

Danny bit his lip. "Look," he said, "if I was a chicken, I'd have made sure you didn't know it was my writing, wouldn't I?"

Scott stood still for a moment. He could see the logic in Danny's words.

"Well, wouldn't I?" Danny went on.

"Who did write it then?" said Scott as he crouched down and removed the lid from the pot with a coin.

"That's what we've got to find out," said Danny.

Scott dipped his brush into the thick yellow paint. He wiped the drips off on the side of the tin and walked over to the wall. He stretched up as high as he could, but the letters were just out of reach. He turned round.

"I need a bunk up," he said.

Danny and Jack didn't move. Danny folded his arms. "Not until you say you believe me."

Scott stared at him. His fists clenched and unclenched. "All right," he said finally. "I believe you."

"*And* apologise for what you put on the blackboard," Danny added.

Scott didn't answer.

"I'm waiting," said Danny.

But Scott was no longer looking at him. He was staring back towards the front gates where twenty or so boys and girls had just come running into the rec. Danny and Jack turned to see. As the kids got nearer, Danny saw that they were all from their class.

"What are *they* doing here?" said Jack.

"As if you didn't know!" Scott shouted. "You told them to come, didn't you? To make sure everyone read your message. You rotten—"

"I didn't tell anyone," Danny shouted. "Except Jack."

"And *I* didn't," said Jack quickly as the other two turned on him. "How could I?"

"Well, *someone* did!" Scott yelled.

"Yeah," said Danny. "Whoever wrote the message in the first place."

Scott stared at him for a second. Then he looked back at the kids running towards them. They were making so much noise – whooping and whistling – that everyone else in the park was coming to join them. Something was going on, and they wanted to know what.

"Come on," said Danny, bending down. "Get up on my back. Let's get that wall painted quick."

Scott didn't argue. He did not want the others seeing the message. By the time the first of the kids were close enough to read the words, MORONE had already vanished under a thick coat of yellow paint. A shout went up.

"Scott Marley is a what?" somebody yelled.

"A numpty!" someone else replied.

"A loser!" said Wes Hunter.

"A captain who scores for the other side," Max Novak suggested, and the sound of taunting laughter filled the air.

Danny ignored them. With Scott still on his back, Danny slowly crawled along the bottom of the wall. Scott painted out the words that were left.

"So, what did it say, Danny?" Luke Edwards called out.

"Yeah, tell us!" everyone shouted.

"What's the point of getting us all up here if you're not going to tell us?"

Scott froze. "So you *did* tell them," he said.

"I didn't," Danny said. Once again it looked as if things were getting out of

control. Danny twisted his head round and looked up at Scott. "Honest, I didn't."

Without a word, Scott painted out the last two letters. The message had gone. But not his anger. As he stepped down, he dipped his brush into the paint one last time. Then, before Danny could straighten up, Scott slapped the thick yellow paint, *splat*, down on Danny's head and ran the brush right the way down his back.

Danny leaped up. "What are you playing at?" he screamed, and shoved Scott back against the wall.

"Whassup?" Scott jeered, and dunked the brush in the paint again. He held it up in front of Danny. "Want a yellow belly as well?"

Danny rubbed at the back of his head. His hair was covered in the slimy paint. He looked at his hand.

"You're crazy!" he yelled. "If I'd written it, why would I need to come and look at it with Jack? I'd have known what it said. And why would I bring everyone else up here? I could have told them at school."

"Yeah, very clever," Scott sneered. "You've got all the answers, haven't you? Almost had me fooled." He turned to the others. "He reckons one of you lot did it."

"Oh, yeah – who?" someone said.

"Typical!" said somebody else.

Danny stared round at the angry faces. There was nothing he could do or say.

"Why don't you just clear off?" said Scott. "You're not welcome here. And you too," he said, turning on Jack.

"But ..." Jack began.

"Jog on," said Scott.

Danny and Jack looked at each other. They had no choice. They walked away with their heads down. The sound of booing and hissing rang in their ears. It was like being at a pantomime – and *they* were the baddies.

They were on the far side of the rec before either of them spoke.

"I'm sorry," said Danny. "I didn't want to drag you into this."

"It's OK," said Jack. "It'll blow over." He sighed. "You know, the more I think about this, the more clever it is. All three of us are being set up."

"How do you mean?" asked Danny.

"Well, think about it. We made sure Scott got to be captain, didn't we?"

"Yeah," said Danny. "You and me."

Jack nodded. "But he's not going to stay captain for long if he's not careful, is he? And then who takes over?"

Danny shrugged. "It *should* have been me. Or you," he added, and grinned.

"Right," said Jack. "But not any more. Whoever wrote that message about Scott has got all three of us into trouble. And who'd vote for you or me now?"

Danny shook his head sadly. They could still hear the sound of far-off booing. "No one," he said.

"Right again," said Jack. "And do you know the worst of it?" he said. "By copying your handwriting, the person who *did* write it has also split the three of us up."

Jack was right. Whoever had written that first message above the goalposts hadn't had to do anything else. Scott had done it all for him. And that *was* clever!

"Which means," Jack went on. "That we'll end up with Max as captain ..."

"Or Wes ..."

"Or Luke Edwards!" they said together, and groaned.

The two boys walked on in silence. The nearer to home Danny got, the more nervous he felt.

"Oh, blimey," Danny moaned. "Mum is going to go mad about the paint! And then they're going to get that letter tomorrow ..." He looked round. "I think I'll go round to my grandad's. *He'll* know what to do."

Chapter 7

"Danny!" his grandad exclaimed as he opened the door. "What a lovely surprise. Come in, come in and ... Oh dear, what's happened?!" He stared at Danny's hair. "Been doing a spot of DIY?"

Danny turned round and showed him the streak of yellow paint down his back. Grandad tutted. "This looks serious," he said. "What have you been up to?"

"It's a long story," Danny muttered.

"It looks like it," his grandad replied, and sighed. "Right then. Give me your sweatshirt.

I'll stick it in a bucket to soak – lucky it's only emulsion paint. Then go and wash your hair. And I'll call your mother to let her know where you are. OK?"

"OK, Grandad," said Danny. And as he ran up the stairs, he already felt better. Grandad Thompson had a way of taking control. Often, it could be a pain in the neck. But sometimes – like now – it felt wonderful.

By the time Danny washed his hair for the third time, most of the paint had gone. Downstairs again, he sat with his grandad at the kitchen table.

"OK then," Grandad said. "So, why don't you start at the beginning?"

And that was exactly what Danny did. He told his grandad everything. "And it wasn't my fault!" he blurted out as his story came to an end. "I didn't do anything! The worst of it is, if we don't sort ourselves out – as a team – we're never going to win the cup. And we've got to!"

Danny's grandad didn't say a word as he thought about what Danny had told him. "And you definitely didn't write on the wall about Scott?" he said.

"No, Grandad," said Danny, looking straight into his eyes. "I swear I didn't."

The old man nodded. "And he called you a chicken, eh?"

"*And* wrote it on the blackboard!" Danny said. "When I get my hands on him, I'll—"

His grandad cut him short. "Not a good idea, Danny," he said. "Not a good idea at all. That's the way wars start. No. What we need here is a truce, not more conflict." He grinned. "And I think I know just what to do. The Chicken and the Egg."

Danny stared at his grandad. "The Chicken and the Egg," he repeated. "What's that?"

Grandad smiled. "Another long story," he said, his eyes twinkling. "Many years ago," he began, "when I was a little bit younger than you are now, something very much like this happened in the street where I lived."

"What?" said Danny. "Someone called you a chicken?"

"No, not me," said Grandad. "A boy called Archie Tucker. But it was my grandfather who sorted it all out. Now *there* was a wise old man. You'd have loved him, Danny. Anyway," he said, and he took a deep breath. "It was all a misunderstanding – the result of people just not listening to each other. A boy called Walter something-or-other called Archie a chicken – for something he hadn't done."

"Just like me," said Danny.

"Archie attacked."

"Just like me!"

"Walter counter-attacked."

Danny grinned. "Just like Scott," he said.

"Archie counter-counter-attacked," his grandad said. "And so it went on."

"Just like us," Danny laughed.

"Oh, far worse," his grandad said. "It turned really nasty. I remember one afternoon, Walter went into Archie's house and emptied the feathers from two pillows all over Mrs Tucker's front room. She went mad! Then Archie set fire to Walter's blazer. Then Walter and a couple of friends grabbed Archie after school and wrote CHICKEN across his forehead with a permanent marker. Then Archie ..." He paused. "In short, it got totally out of hand."

Danny sat and listened. It was odd to think of his grandfather as a boy, and odder still to hear that Grandad had been in the middle of an argument so like his own.

"And of course," Grandad went on, "in those days, we all played out in the road. Hardly any cars, you see. So you couldn't afford to fall out with anyone. After all, everyone knew everyone else. You had to see them every day. That's how my grandfather got to know. He understood what was going on – and he came up with a plan to sort things out, once and for all."

"The Chicken and the Egg," said Danny.

"Precisely," said Grandad, and chuckled.

"So, what *is* it?" asked Danny.

"Hang on," his grandad said. "That's what I'm just coming to."

As Danny listened to his grandad, a grin spread slowly over his face. The plan was brilliant.

"It's perfect," he said at last. "But why should Scott go along with it?"

"Greed," Grandad told him.

"And what if he guesses …?"

"He won't," said Grandad. "No one ever does. Trust me."

Chapter 8

At half past ten the next morning, Danny and Jack were up the rec again, on their bikes.

"The thing is," Danny was saying, "Grandad reckons that you've got the most important job. It's up to you to explain the ground rules so that everyone understands. The fighting must stop." He looked around. "You did text Scott, didn't you?"

Jack nodded. "It's all set. He'll be here at eleven."

"Good," said Danny. "Now, are you sure you know what you've got to say?"

"I think so," said Jack. "Let's just run through it one more time."

"I can do better than that," said Danny. "Grandad wrote down the main points. Here," he said. He pulled a piece of paper from his kit-bag and handed it to Jack. "Read this."

*

At eleven on the dot, Scott arrived. He jumped off his bike and walked up to the other two.

"So, what's all this about?" he said. "You made it sound important."

"It is," said Jack as he slipped the notes into his back pocket. "The thing is, you and Danny have reached a stalemate," he said.

"A what?" said Scott.

"Stalemate," said Danny. "We're stuck – both of us thinking the other one is in the wrong."

Scott grunted.

"This all started because you wouldn't believe Danny didn't write that graffiti," said Jack. "Now, since he can't prove he didn't, and since we can't make you change your mind, we've ... errm, thought up a plan for a truce."

"What sort of plan?" asked Scott angrily.

"We've got to stop being enemies!" said Danny. "It's not getting us anywhere."

"Yeah, well, if you hadn't—"

Jack raised his hands and called for quiet. "The name of the plan," he announced, "is the Chicken and the Egg."

Scott grinned. "Sounds about right," he said.

"Exactly," said Jack. "Since you accused Danny of being a chicken, it is right and proper that he should use eggs to bring the conflict to an end."

Danny reached into his bag and pulled out an egg box. He flipped open the lid. There were two eggs inside. Scott looked at them and sniggered.

"What are they for?" he said.

"That's what I'm about to tell you," said Jack. "Now listen, and listen carefully."

"Go on then," said Scott.

"The offer is this," he said. "Danny will give you ten pounds if you let him break two eggs on your head."

Scott stared at him and Danny. "You two must think I'm mental!" he said. "Why should I agree to that?"

"Ten pounds?" said Danny.

Scott fell silent.

"The thing is," said Jack, "if you decide to go ahead, you must agree that this marks the end of the conflict."

Scott looked at Danny and gave a confused shrug.

"He means that whatever happens, after this we're quits," said Danny. "It's over."

"And this is why," Jack added, working hard to remember the notes Danny's grandad had written out. "One. Because he planned this meeting, you can see Danny is not acting behind your back. And if you accept his offer ..." He laughed. "On your head be it!"

"And if I don't?" said Scott.

"He's still proved that he's not a chicken," said Jack. "Two. If you do say yes, Danny will have got his own back for what you did

yesterday with the paint, and he agrees not to take the matter any further."

"Three," Jack continued. "The ten pounds ..."

"Yeah, yeah," said Scott. "The ten pounds. I know. That's to make me agree." He stared at Jack. "What's the catch?"

Jack wanted to grin, but he kept a straight face as he spoke. "Danny will give you ten pounds if you let him break two eggs on your head," he said for a second time. "That's it."

"Where's the ten pounds?" asked Scott.

Danny pulled out a crisp ten-pound note from his back pocket and held it out for Scott to inspect.

"Where did you get that?" Scott asked.

"My grandad gave it to me this morning," Danny said. "It's for real. It's his idea. The truce and everything."

Scott was puzzled. The plan seemed foolproof, but he still felt sure it must be a trick.

In the meantime, other kids in the park had noticed Scott, Jack and Danny together. Given the fun and games yesterday, they came to investigate. And when Luke Edwards and Max Novak rolled up on their bikes and saw something was going on, they rode over too.

"What's happening?" Luke asked a girl in the crowd.

"*That* boy," she said, pointing to Danny, "is going to give *that* boy ten pounds if he lets him smash two eggs on his head."

Luke smiled. "Is he now?" he said. Like everyone else, he thought he'd stay to find out what would happen next.

"Well?" said Jack.

Scott stopped and looked up. He'd gone through the offer a hundred times in his head. Whichever way he looked at it, he was going to end up ten quid better off. How could he lose? He looked Jack in the face.

"All right," he said. "You're on."

Jack smiled. "Good decision," he said. "Now, before we start you've both got to agree that whatever happens, this is it. The end of the fighting."

Danny and Scott stared at one another. They nodded.

"Shake on it then," said Jack.

Danny stuck his hand out. Scott waited for a moment, then shook it.

"Right," said Jack. "Scott, kneel down. Danny, take the two eggs and stand behind him."

The crowd of children whispered and giggled as Danny and Scott took up their positions. Jack looked at his watch.

"It is eleven-thirty," he said. "Let the Chicken and the Egg begin."

Chapter 9

The boys and girls went silent. Danny looked
down at the two eggs, one in his right hand,
one in his left. Meanwhile, Scott stared ahead,
ready for what was about to happen.

Suddenly, the waiting was over. With a flick
of his wrist, Danny brought the right-hand egg
down on Scott's head. A cheer went up as the
shell smashed. It was followed by squeals of
laughter as slimy white and gooey yolk trickled
down over Scott's head and cheeks. One stray
blob slithered down the back of his neck.

Scott screwed his face up but still stared
ahead. *It isn't* that *bad*, he thought. *One down,*

one to go. Normally, if he wanted extra money for something, he had to earn it. Wash the car, mow the lawn: that sort of thing. This was going to be the easiest ten pounds he'd ever made.

And yet, as one or two in the crowd began to snigger, Scott began to have the horrible feeling that he'd missed something. He shifted about on his knees as he waited for the next egg.

"Come on then," he said. "Get it over with."

Danny didn't reply. And when he looked round, Scott saw that both he and Jack were trying their best not to laugh.

"The second egg," he said angrily. "Are you going to break it on my head, or what?"

"No," said Danny, simply. "No, I'm not."

The crowd of children began to laugh out loud. One by one, those who hadn't understood what was going on had it explained to them by those who had. In the end, Scott was the only person left who still didn't understand.

"Go on!" he shouted. "That was the deal."

"No it wasn't," someone yelled out from the crowd.

"The offer was that Danny would give you ten pounds if you let him break two eggs on your head," Jack said. "*Two* eggs."

"I know that," said Scott. "And I said he could." He twisted round to Danny. "So, get on with it."

"No," Danny repeated. "I only feel like breaking *one* egg."

Suddenly, Scott clicked. He jumped up, mad. "You tricked me!" he screamed as he leaped at Danny.

But Jack was ready for him. He grabbed Scott's arm and, with some others from the crowd, held him back.

"You agreed not to do anything else," Jack told him. "Whatever happened!"

"Anyway," said Danny. "You weren't tricked. You were outwitted."

Scott stared at Danny. Then at Jack. He knew they were right. It was his fault for letting the promise of the money get in the way. They'd told him everything – but he just hadn't seen it. The whole thing was clever. Very clever. Suddenly, his face broke into a huge grin.

"You got me, didn't you?" he said.

"Fair and square," said Danny. "Truce?"

Scott nodded. "Truce," he said.

Once again, a cheer went up from the crowd of spectators. Danny pulled a towel from his bag, and Scott took it. He rubbed it over his head and round his face and neck. Then he turned to the cheering crowd and bowed.

Only one person seemed unhappy. He glared at the three boys – who were friends again now.

"You really *are* a moron, aren't you?" he called out.

Scott looked round. It was Luke Edwards. "What did you say?"

"You heard," said Luke.

"Did you say I was a moron? Spell that for me!" said Scott slowly. "Does it have an 'e' at the end?"

Luke turned bright red. He knew he'd made a mistake.

"Yeah. I mean, that's what Danny called you, isn't it? S'what he sprayed on the wall. That's what I heard," Luke went on. "I mean, that's what he told me."

With each word, Luke was landing himself deeper and deeper in it. If only he'd kept his mouth shut!

"It was *you*!" Scott yelled. "How did you know that's what the graffiti said? I painted over it before anyone else saw."

Luke began to back away.

"*You* wrote it!" said Scott. "You started all of this. YOU!"

"I told you," Danny said to Jack.

"Where's that other egg?" Scott roared.

"Here," said Danny.

Seeing what was about to happen, Luke turned on his heels and raced off. Scott and Jack jumped onto their bikes and sped after him, with Danny – egg in hand – bringing up the rear. Luke was fast but not fast enough to escape three boys on bikes. As he raced down the slope at the far corner, he found Jack blocking his way. He stopped. Danny skidded to a halt to his right; Scott, to his left.

The three of them got off their bikes and ran towards him. Luke didn't know what to do. Suddenly, he made a dash for it. At least, he tried to. The next moment he had tripped over Jack's leg and ended up sprawled out on the grass.

Scott was on him at once. He rolled him over and pinned his arms down with his knees. Luke tried kicking him, but Scott soon put a stop to that by sitting back on his legs.

Danny walked over slowly. He knelt down and clamped Luke's head still with his knees.

Then he held the second egg against Luke's forehead.

"Oh, don't," Luke moaned. "You've got it all wrong."

"I don't think so," said Danny.

Scott looked up at Danny. "Go on then," he said.

"I thought you'd want to help," Danny said.

Scott grinned. "Too right!" he said. And, with Danny and Scott pressing lightly down on the egg, Jack began the countdown.

"Ten, nine, eight, seven, six, five, four ..."

The two boys increased the pressure on the egg.

"... three, two, one."

Splat!

The shell shattered. The egg splattered. The slimy goo slid down into Luke's eyes, his ears, his mouth.

"You sad losers!" he spluttered.

Danny moved his knees apart; Scott let go and stood up. Luke stayed on the grass.

Scott stared down at him. "Now we're *all* quits," he said. "But if you ever pull a stunt like that again ..."

"Let's go," said Jack quietly. "He isn't worth it."

As they wheeled their bikes away, they passed the boys and girls who were just arriving to see what had happened.

"Is it all over?" they asked.

"Yeah," said Jack. "All over his face!"

Danny and Scott laughed.

"What shall we do now?" said Scott.

Danny stopped and reached into the kit-bag. He pulled out his football, threw it up and kicked it high in the air. He grinned.

"We haven't played Corner for a while," he said.

Scott let his bike drop. "Race you to the goal," he shouted.

Chapter 10

Two Wednesdays later, Danny's grandad was watching his grandson play in the replay of the Langton Town Junior Cup, being held at Weston Juniors. He was standing on the touchline near the centre of the pitch, bellowing his support.

"Come on, Dale! You can do it, lads!" he roared.

The team couldn't have played better. Passing, dribbling, attacking, defending – they looked like true professionals. Not once did Danny find himself undefended. Not once did Scott hog the ball. In fact the only goal of the first half came when he cut short a run down the left wing and chipped the ball over to Luke Edwards, who headed it into the far corner of the net.

At the beginning of the second half, it looked as if Weston were about to equalise. Their number 2 struck a nasty dipping shot from way outside the penalty area. It was heading for the top right corner of the goal. Danny watched it, arms out. The ball hurtled down. At the last moment, Danny jumped and flew across the goalmouth to meet it.

Would he make it?

The next instant, the ball thudded against his fingers. Catching it was impossible. All Danny could hope to do was push it over the bar for a corner.

As he fell to the ground, a cheer went up around the pitch. For a second Danny feared that the goal had gone in after all.

He looked up. No, he realised. It was the Dale lot who were cheering. He'd done it!

"Bravo, Danny!" his grandad roared.

As he sped up the pitch minutes later, Jack passed the ball to Scott, who booted it far up the field to a running Wes Hunter. Wes slipped it past their number 6 and kicked it on. The ball floated back towards the goal. Scott was ready and waiting – and onside.

Boof!

He booted the ball on the volley, smack bang into the middle of the net. The goalie never stood a chance.

Ten minutes before the end, Scott scored again. And Jack's goal – in the eighty-fifth minute – made it 4–0. When the final whistle blew, a roar of victory went up. Dale had done it. They'd won. The Langton Town Junior Cup was theirs!

First on the pitch was Mr Croft, then Danny's grandad. "Well done, lads! You did us proud!" they both shouted.

Danny, who along with Scott, Jack and Luke was up on his team-mates' shoulders, looked down. He saw his grandad grinning up at him.

"We did it, Grandad!" he yelled.

"You definitely did," his grandad called back. He winked. "With a little bit of help."

"Yeah. I ... *Whooaah!*" Danny roared with laughter as the boys carrying him lurched to the left. He turned back to his grandad. "I'll see you later," he shouted as he held on tight to his friends' shoulders. "And thanks!"

Danny's grandad smiled as his grandson was carried off across the playing field. "Don't thank me," he said, and laughed. "Thank the Chicken and the Egg."